A NOTE TO PARENTS

When your children are ready to "step into reading," giving them the right books is as crucial as giving them the right food to eat. **Step into Reading Books** present exciting stories and information reinforced with lively, colorful illustrations that make learning to read fun, satisfying, and worthwhile. They are priced so that acquiring an entire library of them is affordable. And they are beginning readers with a difference—they're written on five levels.

Early Step into Reading Books are designed for brand-new readers, with large type and only one or two lines of very simple text per page. **Step 1 Books** feature the same easy-to-read type as the Early Step into Reading Books, but with more words per page. **Step 2 Books** are both longer and slightly more difficult, while **Step 3 Books** introduce readers to paragraphs and fully developed plot lines. **Step 4 Books** offer exciting nonfiction for the increasingly independent reader.

The grade levels assigned to the five steps—preschool through kindergarten for the Early Books, preschool through grade 1 for Step 1, grades 1 through 3 for Step 2, grades 2 through 3 for Step 3, and grades 2 through 4 for Step 4—are intended only as guides. Some children move through all five steps very rapidly; others climb the steps over a period of several years. Either way, these books will help your child "step into reading" in style!

For my brother-in-law,
Doug,
who introduced me to Bruno
–F.W.

To Mom and Dad
–B.S.

Text copyright © 1999 by Ferida Wolff. Illustrations copyright © 1999 by Brad Sneed.
All rights reserved under International and Pan-American Copyright Conventions.
Published in the United States by Random House, Inc., New York, and simultaneously
in Canada by Random House of Canada Limited, Toronto.

www.randomhouse.com/kids

Library of Congress Cataloging-in-Publication Data
Wolff, Ferida. Watch out for bears! / by Ferida Wolff ; illustrated by Brad Sneed.
p. cm. — (Step into reading. A step 2 book)
SUMMARY: Henry and Bruno the bear become friends and they share Henry's honey, Henry's house, and
a camping trip. ISBN 0-679-88761-X (pbk.). — ISBN 0-679-98761-4 (lib. bdg.) [1. Bears–Fiction.
2. Friendship — Fiction.] I. Sneed, Brad, ill. II. Title. III. Series: Step into reading. Step 2 book.
PZ7.W82124Wat 1999 [E]–dc21 97-21419

Printed in the United States of America 10 9 8 7 6 5 4 3 2 1

STEP INTO READING is a registered trademark of Random House, Inc.

Step into Reading®

Watch Out for BEARS!

The Adventures of
Henry and Bruno

By Ferida Wolff • Illustrated by Brad Sneed

A Step 2 Book

Random House 🏠 New York

Chapter 1
Honey for Bruno

Henry loved honey.

He put honey on his waffles.

He put honey on his pancakes.

He put honey on his toast.

When his honey jar was empty,

he went to town to get more.

The road to town

was long and bumpy.

Henry said,

"If I had bees,

I wouldn't have to go to town."

So he set up a hive in the meadow
near his garden.
"Now I will have honey
whenever I want it," he said.

One day

Henry saw something move

in the meadow.

It was big and dark.

Each day the big, dark something

came a little closer.

Henry *knew* it was a bear—

a big, hairy bear.

Henry was worried about his honey.

All day long he kept watch.

Once, he heard something
in the bushes.

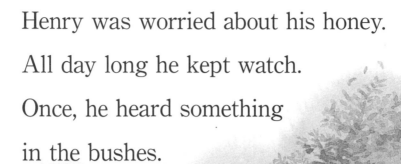

Once, he saw something
by the woodpile.

Henry grabbed a broomstick.
"No bear is going to get
this honey!" he said.
Henry slept on the porch
instead of in his bed.

In the morning
the bear wasn't in the bushes.
It wasn't by the woodpile.

It was face to face with Henry!

Henry picked up the broomstick.

"There's no need for that,"

said the bear.

"Who are you?" asked Henry.

"I'm Bruno. Pleased to meet you,"

said the bear.

Henry remembered his honey.

He rushed over to the hive.

"I didn't take your honey,"

said Bruno.

"What kind of bear

do you think I am?"

"A honey-loving bear,"

said Henry.

"That's true," said Bruno.

"But I wouldn't touch a drop

of that honey without being asked."

Bruno smiled and said,

"Are you asking?"

"No," said Henry.

Bruno moved closer to the hive.

"Honey tastes better

on waffles, anyway," Bruno said.

"It's good on toast, too."

Henry began to get hungry.

Bruno wiggled the hive a little.

The bees buzzed.

One angry bee came out.

"Leave that hive alone,"

said Henry.

"Whatever you say," said Bruno.

He bumped the hive

as he turned away.

Many angry bees came out.

They swarmed around Henry.

"*Shoo,*" said Henry.

He waved his broomstick.

The broomstick smacked

against the hive.

"Oh, no!" Henry cried.

"There goes my honey."

Bruno stretched out his arm.

He caught the hive

in his big, hairy paw.

"You saved my honey," said Henry.

"So I did," said Bruno.

"Well, I guess I'll be going,"
Bruno said.

"Hey, Bruno. I'm asking,"
said Henry.

"How do you like your pancakes?"

Bruno followed Henry inside.

"With honey on top," said Bruno.

Chapter 2
Bruno Finds a Home

Plippety, plop. Ploppety, plip.

"This cave is too damp," said Bruno.

"I need a new home."

He tramped up the hill.

Henry was weeding his garden.

"What's new, Bruno?" he said.

"My cave leaks," said Bruno.

"I have to move."

Henry brushed off his hands.

"I'll help you find a new home,"
he said.

In the forest they noticed

a hollow tree trunk.

"How about this, Bruno?"

asked Henry.

Bruno squeezed into the tree.

He couldn't sit down.

He couldn't turn around.

"No good," he said.

"I need a big house

like yours, Henry."

They discovered a cave.

"This cave is big," said Henry.

Bruno went into the cave

and came running out.

"Bats," he said.

"I can't live in a dirty bat cave.

I want a clean house

like yours, Henry."

Deeper in the forest
they found an old cabin.
"It's too plain," said Bruno.
"I want a house with a front porch
like yours, Henry."

Bruno sat on an old log and sighed.
"I wonder if I will *ever* find
   the right place to live."
"Let's see," Henry said.
"You want a big, clean, dry house
   with a porch."
"Yes," said Bruno.
"Then I know just the place,"
   said Henry.

They walked through the forest
until they came to a meadow.

They walked through the meadow
until they came to a garden.

They walked through the garden
until they came to a house.

"This is *your* house, Henry,"
said Bruno.
"Yes," said Henry.
"My house is dry.
It is clean.
It has a front porch.
And it is big—
big enough for two."

"Would you like to come
live with me, Bruno?"
Bruno gave Henry a bear hug.
"Your house *does* have everything
I want," he said.
"And it has one thing more."
"What is that?" asked Henry.
"Your house has a friend,"
said Bruno.

Chapter 3
Watch Out for Bears

Henry was almost all packed.

"Where are you going, Henry?"

Bruno asked.

"Camping," said Henry.

"You mean you'll sleep

and eat outdoors?"

"Yes," said Henry.

"And you'll swim and catch fish?"

"Right," Henry said.

"I used to do that," said Bruno.

"I think I'll go along
  for old times' sake."

Off they went into the forest.

Bruno knew the best trails

from his cave bear days.

They hiked and ate gorp—

*g*ood *o*ld *r*aisins and *p*eanuts.

After a while they came

to a stream.

"Let's camp here," said Henry.

They set up the tent.

Then they ate lunch.

Bruno patted his full tummy.

"I love camping," he said.

Henry put the rest of the food
into a canvas bag.
He tied a rope to each end.
"Tie that rope to a branch, Bruno,"
said Henry.

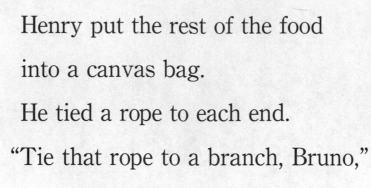

"I'll tie this rope here."
The bag hung high in the air.
"Why did we do that, Henry?"
Bruno asked.

"We have to watch out for bears,"
said Henry.
"A bear might eat our food
if we leave it on the ground."
Bruno agreed.
He didn't want *any* old bear
eating their food.

"Want to swim?" asked Henry.

Bruno raced Henry into the water.

They played water tag.

They floated on their backs

and pretended to be whales.

"Hey, look at all the fish,"

Henry said.

"I'll get my fishing rod."

"Don't bother," said Bruno.

"I will teach you to fish

like a bear."

He scooped a fish from the water.

Henry tried it Bruno's way,

but all he got was wet.

Bruno scooped out more fish.

"You caught the fish,

so I'll make dinner," said Henry.

The fish were delicious!

Bruno thought about the bag of food.

"Do you think that bag is
  sturdy enough, Henry?" he said.

"Bears are strong, you know."

"The bag is strong, too,"
  said Henry.

Soon the stars came out.

Henry pointed to the North Star.

Bruno found the Great Bear.

Henry stretched.

"I'm ready for bed," he said.

"Me too," said Bruno.

Henry fell asleep right away.

But Bruno was wide awake.

Every sound made him think

of bears.

Was their food safe?

He had to check.

Bruno lowered the bag.

He looked inside.

Everything was there.

The chocolate energy bars smelled

good through their wrappers.

He ate one before he tied the bag

to the tree again.

But Bruno still couldn't sleep.

What if a bear was there now?

He shuffled past Henry

for another look.

No bears.

But all that food made Bruno's

stomach growl.

"Maybe I'll just have a little snack,"

he thought.

Bruno had a sandwich and juice.

He ate the last apple

and the rest of the gorp.

Bruno's stomach was full.

His eyelids felt heavy.

Bruno had no trouble

falling asleep in the tent now.

Henry awoke with the sun.

"Bruno, get up," Henry said.

"It's time for breakfast."

There were only empty boxes

and torn wrappers in the bag.

"What happened?" Henry said.

Bruno poked his sleepy head out.

"Bad news, Henry," he said.

"A bear ate our food, after all."

Bruno went back to sleep.

Henry began to clean up.

"Next time I will only watch out

for *one* bear," said Henry.